For Gonzalo (heart and wings),
who knows no borders.
With all my thanks.

Susana

Blue Dot Kids Press
www.BlueDotKidsPress.com

Original English-language edition published in 2020 by Blue Dot Kids Press, PO Box 2344, San Francisco, CA 94126.
Blue Dot Kids Press is a trademark of Blue Dot Publications LLC.

Original English-language edition © 2020 Blue Dot Publications LLC
Original English-language edition translation © 2020 Lawrence Schimel
Text © Susana Gómez Redondo; Illustrations © Sonja Wimmer

Spanish-language edition originally published in Spain under the title *El día que Saída llegó* © 2012 Takatuka SL, Barcelona.
English-language edition arranged through Mundt Agency, Düsseldorf, Germany,
and is published under exclusive license with Takatuka SL, Barcelona.

Original English-language edition edited by Summer Dawn Laurie and designed by Susan Szecsi,
with special thanks to Marcia Lynx Qualey and Ruth Ahmedzai Kemp for adapting and translating the Arabic in this book.

BLUE
DOT

Cataloging in Publication Data is available from the United States Library of Congress.

ISBN: 9781733121255

MIX
Paper from
responsible sources
FSC™ C136333
FSC
www.fsc.org

The illustrations in the book are hand-painted, using acrylic paint and crayons.

Printed in China with soy inks

First Printing

# THE DAY Saida ARRIVED

Written by Susana Gómez Redondo
Illustrated by Sonja Wimmer
Translated by Lawrence Schimel

BLUE DOT KIDS PRESS

The day Saida arrived, it seemed to me that she had lost all her words. So, I tried to look for them in every

nook
cranny corner
drawer
seam

to see if, between them and me, we might get rid of her tears and throw away her silence.

The day Saida arrived, I searched under the tables, the blackboard, and the desks.

I looked through the notebooks and between the colored pencils.

Under the cushions and beneath the book jackets.

Inside the pockets of all the coats.

Between the curtains, the hands of the clock,

and the letters of the stories.

But no matter how hard I tried, I couldn't find any of Saida's words.
When she looked at me with her large amber eyes, I thought
I saw questions and sadness inside her.

The day Saida arrived, I knew
I would always be her friend.

With a finger, I drew a welcome for her,
warm and soft, like long scarves and
fluffy pillows.

She drew a smile for me
like a crescent moon.

After, I kept looking for her words,
to see if between us, the words and me,
we might untie her laughter,
and her voice.

The day Saida arrived,
I looked and looked again
beneath **the park benches.**

In the hollows of **trees.**

**In all the trash cans,**

**swing sets,**

and **fountains.**

Even inside the mouths of statues...

But I didn't find even a trace of Saida's words. Just some banana peels, candy wrappers, the crusts of a sandwich, and an earthworm. So, I painted a hug for her, and she, drying some tears that were just as salty as my own, drew a camel for me where some paint had flaked away.

The day Saida arrived, Mama spoke to me
of a land of bazaars and archways and colorful tiles.
With her finger, she pointed out Saida's country
on the round globe of the world.

## MO-ROC-CO, I could read...

**and I saw that it was right beside the sea.**

The day Saida arrived, Papa explained to me
that my friend surely hadn't lost her words,
but perhaps she didn't want to bring them out
because they were different from the words
we used here.

"In Morocco," he said, "yours wouldn't work either."

That's how I found out that
in Saida's country they
speak a language called

## Arabic.

It was the night
of the day Saida arrived,
as I drew hand shadows of
camels and palm trees on
the wall of my room, that
I decided to help Saida learn
our words, and to ask her
to teach me her own.

That way, when *I* travel to
Morocco someday...

That's how, thanks to Saida and her arrival, she and I learned a world of new words. She pointed to things with her small hands, and I pronounced their names, writing them out on the blackboard, in the sandbox at recess, with notebooks and colored pencils. Then I repeated them slowly so that the sounds would become rooted in her memory and on her lips.

Saida translated them into her language full of *B* sounds and drew them with those letters that sometimes looked like flowers and other times like insects. Then she repeated them slowly so that the sounds would become rooted in my memory and on my lips.

hippopotamus
(jamoos al-bahr)
جاموس البحر

country
(balad)
بلاد

girl
(bint)
بنت

I liked her letters.

I also thought it was fun that things were read

end. the from starting

blue
azraq
أزرق

river
nahr
نهر

bread
khubz
خبز

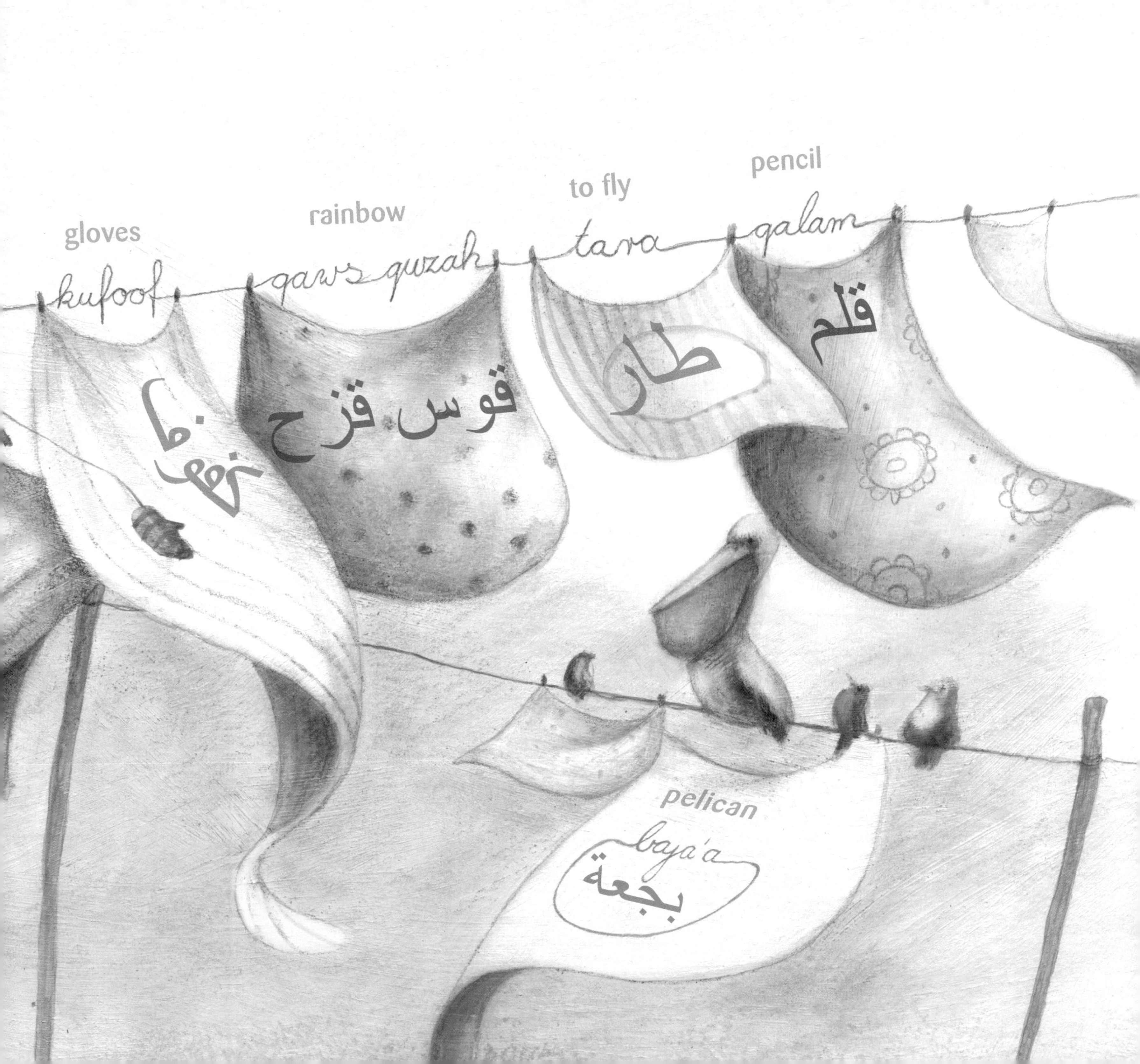

gloves

kufoof

قفاز

rainbow

qaws quzah

قوس قزح

to fly

tara

طار

pencil

qalam

قلم

pelican

baja'a

بجعة

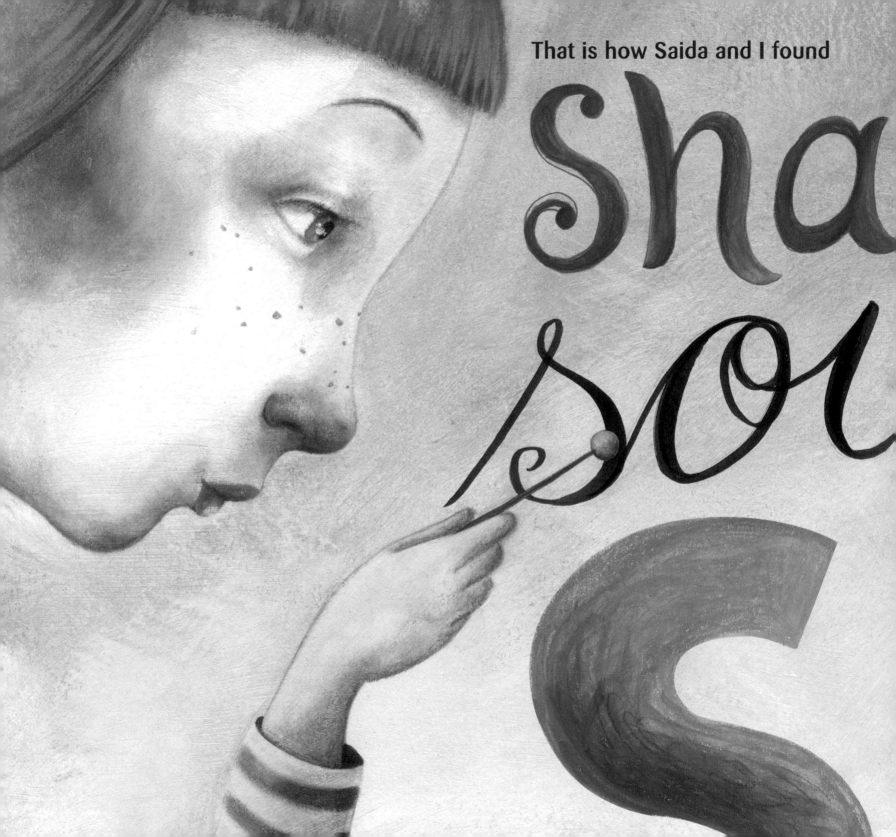

That is how Saida and I found

Some appeared every morning
like a greeting or a good breakfast.
Others were carried off by the wind,
and we never saw them again.
There were some that, forgotten
under the snow or the frost, came back
with the return of good weather
and the thaw.

And we knew that in all languages, there are words
as warm as breath and others cold as metal.

Words that bring together, and words that separate.
Words that cause hurt, words that awaken laughter.
Words that tickle when they're spoken, and others that,
when we hear them, feel like a hug.

Some days, Saida and I painted them different colors
and watched them take flight like birds or butterflies.

Other days, we spread them on the grass, so they could
bathe in the light of the sun, the moon, or the stars.

There were afternoons when we made piles of them and
let ourselves fall into them.

APPLE
(TUFFĀHA)
تفاحة

أحمر
('AHMAR)
RED

MOUNTAIN
spaghetti

FISH (SAMAKA)

HOPE

Saida laughed when she got muddled up between a *P* and a *B*. And I coughed when a *Q* got stuck in my throat! Then she offered me an almond-and-honey sweet to wash it down, and I thrilled her taste buds with a piece of carrot cake.

BOAT

(SAFINA) سفينة

PARTY (HAFLA) حفلة

جبل

(JABAL)

معكرونة

(MA'KARUNA)

SUGAR (SUKKAR)

سكر

سمكة

أمل (AMAL)

CAT (QITT) قط

CLOUDS (GHUYŪM)

غيوم

TREE (SHAJARA) شجرة

TELEPHONE
(HĀTIF)
هاتف

Some time has passed since the day Saida arrived.

Now flowers paint the sidewalks, and the almond trees are so white it looks like they're covered with snow. Now every morning Saida uncovers her voice and her laughter, and from her mouth come

of every Shape, Sound & size.

I still find it funny when my tongue
gets in a tangle trying to roll my *Rs*.
She still laughs when her *Es* sound like *Is*.
Then Saida recites for me a poem by
Jacqueline Woodson, and after, I offer her
a story set in the medina of Marrakech.

Then we go to her house to eat couscous. At mine,
we have peanut butter and jelly sandwiches.

mirror (MIR'ĀT)

summer (SAIF)

pastry (FATA'IR)

submarine

planet (KAWKAB) كوكب journey

carrots (JAZAR) جزر garden (BUSTAN) بستان easy

umbrella (MIZALLA) مظلة

laughter (DAHIK) ضحك

house
(bayt)
بيت

camel
(jamal)
جمل

One day, Saida and I will travel to her land of spices and camels. On our way to Africa, we'll keep watch for more words, to see if, together, we can learn all the ones that unleash laughter, voice, and friendship.

And on that day, Saida and I will happily throw overboard unwelcome words like

*b*

*o*

*r*

# English Alphabet

A a    B b    C c    D d

E e    F f    G g    H h

I i    J j    K k    L l

M m    N n    O o    P p

Q q    R r    S s    T t

U u    V v    W w

X x    Y y    Z z

# Arabic Alphabet

| | | | |
|---|---|---|---|
| ج | ث | ت | ب | ا |
| | | | ح |
| ر | ذ | د | خ | |
| | | | ز |
| ض | ص | ش | س | |
| | | | ط |
| ف | غ | ع | ظ | |
| | | | ق |
| ن | م | ل | ك | |
| | ي | و | ه | |

Did you know that Arabic is written from right to left and the alphabet includes twenty-eight letters?

ﺓ

ﻝ

ي

happy (sa'īda) ﺳﻌﻴﺪﺓ